Peppa Goes Around the World

It was almost the start of the summer holidays. Peppa was playing in the garden with her friends.

"What are you doing over the holidays?"
asked Wendy Wolf.
"I'm going to the park," replied Peppa.
Peppa was very excited. She was going
to spend the holidays jumping in
lots of muddy puddles!

Peppa's friends were going on holiday all around the world.

"I'm going to the **jungle**," said Pedro Pony.

"We're going to the **desert . . .**" said Emily and Edmond Elephant.

"... and I'm going to the **mountains!**" barked Danny Dog.

"What about you, Suzy?" asked Peppa. "I'm off to the **South Pole** to play with the penguins," Suzy Sheep grinned.

On the first day of the holidays,
Peppa and George climbed into the car.
"Time to go the park," said Mummy Pig.
"Let's go!" cheered Daddy Pig.

The little car bounced along the road.
The engine went chugga-chugga-chugga . . .

Bang!

Clang!

Bonk!

"Oh dear," groaned Daddy Pig. "The car has broken down."

Mummy Pig called for help.

"Please come quick," she said. "This is an emergency."

"Look!" gasped Peppa. "Here comes Miss Rabbit's
Emergency Breakdown Service!"

"That was quick," said Mummy Pig.

Miss Rabbit said it would take her all day to put things right.
"But we want to go the park!" cried Peppa.
"Don't worry," replied Miss Rabbit. "While I fix your car,
you can borrow my aeroplane!"
"Air-plane!" George shouted.

Everybody climbed into Miss Rabbit's aeroplane.
Mummy Pig took the controls.
"This is fun!" she said.
"Are we supposed to be flying upside down?" wondered Daddy Pig.
"The ground is in the sky and the sky is on the ground!"
giggled Peppa.

Neooooowww!

It didn't take long for Mummy Pig to
get the hang of aeroplane flying.
"Next stop the park," said Daddy Pig.
"To jump in muddy puddles!"
cried Peppa.

Daddy Pig opened out his map.

"Are we lost as usual?" asked Peppa.

"We are **not** lost!" snorted Daddy Pig.

"I can see some trees. That must be the park."

"Where are the swings and roundabouts?" asked Peppa.
"Hmm . . . " said Daddy Pig. "This looks more like
a jungle than a park."
Peppa gasped. Pedro was on holiday in the jungle!

Mummy Pig pulled the handbrake and the plane fell through the trees, landing on the ground with a bump.

Here was Pedro!
"Hello, Pedro!"
called Peppa.
"Are you having
a nice holiday?"
Pedro nodded.
"It's brilliant. There
are parrots, monkeys
and everything!"

The jungle was fun, but there were no
muddy puddles to jump in.
"Can we visit my other friends on their
holidays around the world?" asked Peppa.
"I don't see why not," said Mummy Pig.

Shoooooom!

It was Daddy Pig's turn to fly the aeroplane.
"Where next?" he said.
"The mountains," said Peppa. "That's where Danny Dog is!"

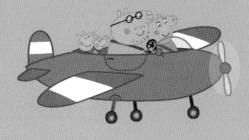

Whhhiirrrr!

Danny Dog was enjoying his
mountain holiday.
"The best bit about climbing
a mountain is that you're
all alone," explained
Captain Dog. "There's no
one else around . . ."

Daddy Pig landed the aeroplane at the top of the mountain, right in front of Danny and Captain Dog.

"Hello, Danny!" shouted Peppa. "We're flying around the world to see my friends. This mountain is very high!"

Peppa and her family said goodbye
to Danny and Captain Dog and flew
away again. Soon, Daddy Pig spotted
lots of yellow sand in the distance.

"It must be the desert," he said.
"That's where Emily and Edmond
are on holiday!" cried Peppa.

It wasn't easy to land an aeroplane in the desert.
"We've sunk into the ground," said Mummy Pig.
"Why do they have to fill the desert with so
much sand?" cried Daddy Pig.
"Hello, Emily!" shouted Peppa. "Hello, Edmond!"

"We've been studying a rare lizard," whispered Edmond, "but it must be shy, because it's run away." "It had a scaly back and a long, red tongue," added Emily.
"Yuck!" said Mummy Pig. "Lucky it ran off then!"

The lizard suddenly appeared on a rock.
"There it is!" shouted Daddy Pig, frightening it away again.
"Did you say you had other people to visit?" sighed Dr Elephant.
"Yes!" said Peppa. "We've still got to go and see Suzy at the South
Pole! Goodbye, everybody!"

Squeak!

Suzy was having a great holiday,
but she did miss Peppa.
"I wish Peppa was here," Suzy sighed.

Skkiiiiddd!
Screech!

Peppa's aeroplane landed on the snow and ice.
"Peppa!" cried Suzy.
"Suzy!" cried Peppa.

Peppa and Suzy were best friends. They were
very pleased to see each other again.

Peppa had lots of fun with Suzy and the penguins, but they couldn't play all day. Peppa still had to go to the park!
"Miss Rabbit should have fixed our car by now," said Mummy Pig.

Whooosh!

The aeroplane flew all the way

back

around

the

world.

"Hello, Miss Rabbit," said Peppa.
"We've flown all around the world!"
"Good thing I remembered to fill the aeroplane's
tank up with petrol this morning," said Miss Rabbit.

"Your little car is working again," said Miss Rabbit.
Peppa and George climbed inside.

Beep!
Beep!

"Flying round the world was nice," decided Peppa,
"but something was missing . . ."

"...a muddy puddle!"

Peppa and George loved jumping up and down in muddy puddles! Everyone loves jumping up and down in muddy puddles!